The Strange Swimming Coach

The Strange Swimming Coach

by

Jerry B. Jenkins

MOODY PRESS

CHICAGO

© 1986 by
JERRY B. JENKINS

ISBN: 0-8024-8238-4

1 2 3 4 5 6 Printing/LC/Year 90 89 88 87 86

Printed in the United States of America

To Jim Ragont

Contents

1
Trouble in the Water

I never thought about getting the Baker Street Sports Club involved in swimming. In fact, it was the last thing on my mind. I liked swimming in the lake in the summertime, but I didn't think I'd like it indoors in the wintertime.

Our school didn't have a pool, so our gym teachers arranged to bus us to another school that did. We all took our little bags full of swimming trunks and towels, and some of the guys brought goggles and even nose plugs.

The ones with nose plugs got razzed by everyone else. "Did you bring your rubber ducky too? Or maybe a boat?"

We all nervously changed and felt strange, padding through a steamy locker room in a school where everyone else was a stranger. When we bunched up at the end of the pool, wondering where to put our towels and whether there was room in the crowded water, we just stood trying to sort of hide behind each other.

It was as if the rest of the swimmers and spectators had all seen us at once. Activity stopped. The echoing noises stopped. All we could see were new faces staring at us. All we could smell was that pungent chlorine and water mixture. And all we could hear was the muffled rush of the water through the filtering system.

Suddenly our coaches and the coaches at the school began barking orders. We were ordered into the water. "Just throw your towels on the benches!" And the swimmers were ordered out. "Make room for the new kids!"

I hadn't had a lot of positive swimming experiences. I mean, I knew how to swim, and I'd spent a lot of hours splashing around in the local swimming hole, but the idea of jumping into one end of an olympic size pool with fifty or sixty other kids my age didn't appeal to me.

I could picture myself bumping into someone or banging heads with someone or winding up beneath someone who wouldn't have room to get out of the way and let me up.

Once, when I had been about seven or eight, I dived off a pier with another kid for a race. He landed right on top of me, and as I struggled to get to the surface, he just kept thrashing, as if trying to win the race.

He was fine. He was on top. He was above the water, breathing freely. I was panicking. I knew enough to hold my breath, but the struggle made it more difficult. I was working harder than I would have been otherwise, and I needed air.

At what seemed the last instant, I struggled free and gasped for breath. He acted as if he had been unaware that I had nearly drowned. And he probably had been.

So now, with everyone else clambering into the pool at the shallow end, I waited with my red, white, and blue towel over my shoulders, just looking around. There was plenty of time. Had I been someone else, the coaches might have hollered at me to get into the pool.

But they knew me. I was an athlete, a good guy, not a trouble maker. I moseyed to the deep end and tossed my towel onto one of the spectator benches. I had never been in a pool area that had so many seats. There must have been a lot of exciting swimming meets there, I decided, and the record board at one end confirmed it.

Some of the other guys had knelt at the edge and splashed water on their pressure points to get used to the shock of the cool water. They splashed the backs of their knees, under their arms, their temples, and their faces. Then they gingerly slid into the water.

I wanted the shock of the cooler water. The pool air was steamy and humid. I was hot even though I had only my trunks on and it was snowing outside. I watched to see how many of the guys would clog up the deep end of the pool.

None did. Apparently they were as cautious as I was after having not swum for so long and not being used to the big pool.

I knew I could dive into the deep end and swim to a point where my feet would reach the bottom. I curled my toes over the edge of the tiled floor and peered down into the clear water. The paint at the bottom made it seem as if you could scoop some water up in your hand and it would look blue.

In black paint at the bottom, a sign read: TWELVE FEET. By the middle of the pool, the depth was five feet. I bent at the waist, threw my arms out ahead of me, and pushed off. I flew out maybe five feet and broke through the water, my feet following my hands underwater, cruising about six feet down before resurfacing.

The shock was total. I loved it. My whole body shuddered, and I breathed out heavily through my nose, groaning with the sensation of it. As I reached the surface for a breath and rolled into an easy freestyle crawl, I was hooked.

It felt great. The movement of the water with all the other guys in it and the rush of the air and purified water and chlorine from the filter gave the pool a buoyancy that seemed to hold me high in the water.

My strokes were effortless, and I seemed to glide quickly toward the middle of the pool. I had never experienced anything like it. I knew I would never want to jump into a pool after preparing myself for the shock. That was one of the best parts.

5

But this ability to roll from side to side, rhythmically kicking, breathing, stroking, cutting through the water! What a thrill!

I soon reached the spot where I could stop and let my legs dangle and touch the bottom, but I didn't want to stop. I pretended to have a purpose, to be trying to prove something, to win a race, break a record, or at least impress someone.

I looked ahead and saw that the way was clear all the way to the shallow end. It was as if it had been prepared just for me, but I knew it was luck and that the way would be clogged up soon if I didn't take advantage of it.

So I surged on through, imagining that everyone was watching me while knowing that probably no one was. In fact, as I picked up speed and glanced from side to side, no one was watching. No coaches, no kids, no one, I thought.

Still, I was inspired. I charged toward the end, trying to remember how it was that the olympians turned. I was feeling a little winded, but I was on a tear now. I had swum fifty meters and wanted to make the flip turn and finish a hundred. I could rest at the other end, even if it was deep. Then I could grab the overhanging lip at the edge of the pool.

I neared the shallow end and took a deep breath. I tucked my head under and did a forward somersault, feeling for the wall with my feet. But I was crooked. I had somehow floated sideways, not knowing what I was doing.

When I straightened my legs out with a mighty thrust, only my left foot hit the wall, but it hit flat and with such power that it did give me a boost to head the other way.

I quickly surfaced and straightened myself out. There was still no one watching that I knew of, but I felt a surge of power go through me and I wanted to speed to the other end. I wondered how fast I was going and whether I had been born to swim. The whole feeling was a surprise to me, but I was loving every second.

As I passed the halfway point again, I was huffing and puffing and thrashing, my feet now lower in the water, my legs feeling leaden and slow, my arms heavy and tight. When I was fully into the deep end, I was suddenly overwhelmed by the feeling that I couldn't go on. I wasn't used to this. Wasn't in shape for it.

I hadn't paced myself, and now I was in trouble. I could hardly move or breathe, but somehow my body kept moving, kept splashing. I slowed to half speed, though I was working just as hard if not harder than ever.

I wanted to just stop and catch my breath, but if I did I would have had to tread water, because I was just as far from the middle as I was to the end or the sides now. The water was ten feet deep. I had to keep going. There was no other choice.

But the thrill, the joy, the fun of it was gone. I nearly panicked. I didn't want to stop and scream for help, even though I shouldn't have let my pride get in my way. It was my secret, my problem. I wanted to handle it. I wanted to somehow reach that overhang where I could hook an elbow up on it and just suspend myself there.

I knew it would be several minutes before I would regain enough strength to pull myself from the pool, so for now the only goal was to reach the end. I really had no idea whether I could make it, but if I didn't I would collapse trying and hope against hope that someone would see me if I dropped to the bottom like a rock.

My eyes were burning from the chlorine, but I stared ahead and caught sight of the edge of my towel hanging over the low wall separating the seats from poolside. I made that my goal. I locked my eyes on it and kept working, kept struggling, kept hanging on.

My lungs felt as if they were about to burst. I tried to make my feet kick, but my legs just hung as dead weights as my arms fought to drag me along. I kept my eye on the corner of the towel, praying that the edge of the pool would come within reach before I gave out.

I became only faintly aware of a lonely figure sitting a few seats away from my towel. Big, deep, brown eyes stared at me intently from a dark face. So, it hadn't been my imagination. Someone *had* been watching.

The big, swarthy face appeared expressionless, but the man with long, slick, black hair combed back over his ears and reaching his collar never took his eyes off me. For a moment I wondered if he was real and if he could see that I was in trouble.

What would he do if I went under? Would he remain there, staring straight through me, that sad, almost scowling look on his face? Would he dive in to save me? Get help? What? I didn't know. With five meters to go, I nearly gave out. My left arm wouldn't follow the stroke of my right.

I rolled to one side and kicked with my feet, and my body drifted almost vertically. With the escaping strength in my right arm, I slapped at the water to stay afloat and to try to make it to the edge.

My head went under. I held what little breath I had. I surfaced and kept fighting. I went down again, this time gulping down a great swallow of water. That was all I needed. I thought I was going to drown.

I thrashed to the surface, both arms and both legs suddenly back in action. I lunged toward the edge and grabbed hold, coughing and spitting out water.

When I realized I was safe and had breathed a prayer of thanks, I looked up toward the dark man. He was sitting back down.

2

The Mysterious Man

So, he *had* seen my crisis. It had brought him to his feet. He had been concerned.

But he sat quickly, almost as if embarrassed that he had stood in the first place. Was that a look of relief on his face, or was I only imagining it? I stared at him.

The look had returned. The bored, impassive, intense, near scowl. He was looking directly at me. I shook my head and smiled, knowing he knew what I meant. He had seen me. He knew. Strangers, we had shared the moment.

His expression didn't change again as he looked directly into my eyes from maybe ten feet away. As my breath and heartbeat returned to normal and that tingly feeling of strength returned to my limbs, I stared back and was startled to see him slowly, solemnly begin to clap.

He clapped in a slow, appreciative booming of his massive hands, and the echoes resounded through the pool. My friends and classmates stopped dead in the water and stared at him. After a half dozen or so claps, he stopped and stood.

He cautiously made his way between the seats to the aisle as everyone but me lost interest in him, and he slowly limped away, seeming to painfully favor his right leg.

He was large but squatty, thick in the thighs, back, chest, and arms. I guessed him to be about fifty and Spanish looking, at least from where I was.

When I was finally able to struggle up onto the deck and head for my towel, I found on it the strangest note on part of a three-by-five card that had been torn in half. Next to a horizontal half circle with teeth was printed in primitive, blocky handwriting, "RATTLESNAKE JAW."

And next to what looked like two upside down V's, one inside the other, was printed, "THUNDERBIRD TRACK."

I was scared. I knew better than to talk to strangers, especially weird ones—as he appeared. But he seemed shy, as if he didn't want to draw attention to himself. The note and the drawings were bizarre. What in the world did they mean?

I slipped the little card into my towel and moved it to the other end of the pool. Then I just waded and bobbed in the shallow end, trying to push from my mind the crisis I'd been through.

Someday, after I'd trained a little and got in shape, I wanted to try it again. And I wanted to be timed. At that point, I didn't even know what a good time would be for a twelve-year-old. But I was going to find out.

I kept glancing up to see if the man would come back. What if he did? Would I have the nerve to approach him? Would he tell me what the note meant? Or was he just mentally ill? Maybe he was from some state facility for the retarded and just liked to visit the pool.

But I was curious. I decided that if I saw him again, I would try to be nice to him and see if I could get him to talk to me. Why not? There were plenty of my friends and adults around.

But he never appeared at the deep end again. I was stunned to see him at the shallow end when it was finally time to get out. I hadn't even looked behind me. He was at the end of the seats near the door and wasn't watching me. He seemed to be studying the record board on the wall.

12

I grabbed my towel and started toward him. "Hey! Mister! Sir?"

If he noticed me, he didn't let on. I thought his eyes met mine, but as I hustled his way, he stood and stepped toward the door, still limping. He hurried out, and a coach hollered at me to get to the showers. Spooky.

A few of the guys asked me who the strange bird was. "Never saw him before in my life."

"You're kiddin', O'Neil! He was clappin' for you! What'd you do, a swan dive or somethin'?"

I shook my head.

Others had their opinion. "He's a nut!"

"Yeah, probably a kidnapper!"

"A mental case."

For some reason I felt like defending him. I didn't say anything, but the man had watched me. He had been concerned enough to stand when I was in trouble. That told me he would have done something—I don't know what—if I hadn't made it to the end.

He *had* appeared to applaud my effort, if not my style. What did it all mean? I had no idea. And if I had never seen him again, I would have forgotten all about it. For now, all I could think of was how invigorating the water and the swimming had been—at least until I had overstepped my abilities.

I couldn't wait to tell the guys in the sports club about it.

That night after dinner we had a meeting scheduled. All the guys were there in our shed near the edge of the back acres. Jimmy Calabresi, my best friend, was a chunky, dark-haired kid who was a good athlete but a slow runner.

Jack Bastable was a huge retarded boy, well over six-feet tall and a tough, hard-hitting, rangy guy whose mind was that of a six- or seven-year-old. We all watched out for him and helped him, and he was one of the stars of the club.

Cory, the red-head, was the only other Christian in the club besides Jimmy and me, but we were working on a few others.

13

Bugsy, our black member, had been to church with us a few times and seemed interested.

The rest of the guys, Ryan, Matt, Toby—another big one—Brent, Andy, Nate, and Kyle, were good kids. We had our arguments, of course, but we had been drawn together by our love for sports and by how close we lived to Baker Street out in the country.

Everyone's father was in some kind of labor trade or farming, except Jimmy's. His dad was a salesman and probably made more money than any of the rest of our fathers, but he had a big family to feed so they didn't seem rich.

Most of the guys weren't impressed with my swimming story, but of course I hadn't told them about the mysterious man. All I said was that swimming in an indoor pool was so much fun that we just had to see if we could enter a team in some competition.

"All we know how to do is splash around near Big Rock Lake, Dallas!"

"Yeah! I couldn't even tell ya what all the events are. And none of us know how to dive."

I was earnest. "Forget the diving! We can learn to swim fast! Maybe we can find a coach somewhere, study some books, practice a lot. That's been the story of this club all along. We find a sport we like, we learn it, we practice it, and we jump in. Now this time we can really jump in!"

Toby was unconvinced. "You're the only one who likes this sport, Dal."

I nodded. "That's only because you haven't tried it! Give it a chance."

"How we supposed to do that?"

"There's an open night of swimming at that pool tomorrow night. The admission charge is small and—"

Little blond Ryan, who looked a lot like Brent, shook his head. "That leaves me out. I don't care if it's ten cents. I won't be able to go."

I assured him we'd pay his way. "Let's all go! It's not that

14

far, and I hear it's not crowded on a school night. It closes at eight, so we wouldn't be out late."

No one smiled or seemed excited about it, but a few reluctantly agreed to go. Most of them told me privately that they thought swimming was a sissy sport, that it wasn't as important as the more well-known sports like baseball, basketball, and football. All I knew was, once they were in the water, they'd love it.

Then I told them about the man. They were wide-eyed and quiet.

"Sounds spooky. Count me out."

"Me too. I don't want to get kidnapped."

"Or killed."

I waved them off. He might have been a nut, but he was concerned about me when I was in trouble. And he clapped for me when I made it.

Seven of us went the next night: Cory, Jimmy, Jack, Ryan, Bugsy, Brent, and I. We all had a good time except Jack. He was afraid of the water and spent most of his time sitting at the edge of the shallow end, his legs dangling in the water. Occasionally we were able to coax him into walking into the pool until the water got up to his chest.

By the end of the evening, he was romping and splashing in the shallow end, but he had no interest in learning to swim. "I will take care of the stuff if you guys start a team, OK, Dallas?"

I nodded.

The rest of us played and swam and were generally rowdy without getting ourselves into trouble. Cory spent a lot of time studying the record board, asking me what the various strokes were like. "What's the breaststroke? I think I know what the backstroke is. And what's the butterfly?"

I shrugged. "I've seen them on television, but that's what we'd have to study if we were going to start a team."

"Jimmy looked quickly at me. "You're not still thinkin' of that, are you?"

15

I nodded.

"I mean, we're all havin' fun and everything, but I hear that swimming is one of the most demanding, grueling sports there is. Who needs that during the school year?"

"Guys who call themselves members of a sports club, that's who. I'll bet you'd be a good competitive swimmer."

He turned away and looked at the board again. "People can swim two hundred yards in just over two minutes? I can't believe it."

"Sure. Older kids, ones who have been training all their lives."

"Do you really think so, Dallas?"

"Think what?"

"That I would be a good swimmer?"

"Sure."

Then we noticed him. At the other end. Sitting, brooding, watching, staring. It was the big, dark, scary man.

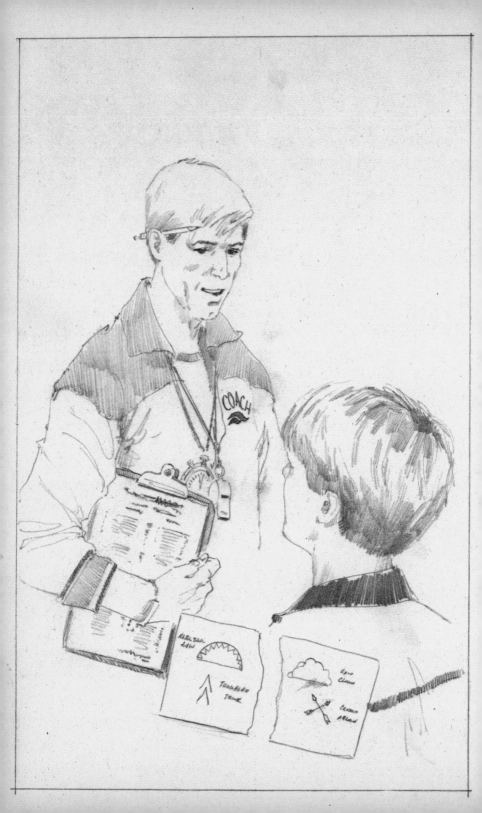

3

More Cryptic Symbols

I knew from experience that if I approached the man, he would hurry away. But what if I swam toward him? What if I swam my fastest? He seemed to like to watch swimming and appreciated a good performance.

I knew I could swim one length of the pool without tiring. In fact, I knew if I gave it all I had and pushed as hard as I could, I could swim one length fairly fast and wind up at the shallow end where I wouldn't be in trouble, even if I was exhausted.

Without a word to Jimmy, I rushed to the edge, bent over, and sprang into the water. I wasn't pacing myself, wasn't breathing correctly, and probably wasn't stroking the best either.

But I was flying. My feet were coming too far out of the water and water was splashing everywhere, but I felt wonderful. It was fun. It was exciting. And as I stole a glance at the man in the seats, I could tell he was staring intensely at me.

Why did I care to impress him? What if he was a criminal? I kept swimming.

With about ten yards to go to the shallow end, I quit breathing and put all my effort into speeding. When I smashed into

Jack Bastable and knocked him under, I realized my mistake.

He came up panicky, yelling and sputtering. I hollered an apology and helped him stand upright. Grief, he was huge. As soon as he felt safe he began to laugh, long and hard. That made me laugh.

When I sneaked a peek at my spectator, he was staring right at us, a big hand over his mouth as if he might have been hiding a smile. I had never seen him smile. And I doubted I ever would.

When it was time to leave, the man was gone. I grabbed my towel and headed for the locker room, but Bugsy called after me. "Hey, Dallas! Something fell out of your towel!"

I had almost missed it. It was another half card with two symbols drawn on it. The first was a primitive cloud with the words RAIN CLOUDS printed next to it. The other was a sketch of arrows in the shape of an X. The printing read: CROSSED ARROWS.

Now I was genuinely scared. Clearly, the man was trying to communicate with me. And I had no idea who he was, what he was trying to say, or whether I even really wanted to know.

The guys were all intrigued now. They had enjoyed the swimming and wanted me to look into how and where we could compete, but they were more interested in the mysterious man.

No one could have predicted where our first clue would come from, but it happened the next afternoon, after school in the clubhouse. We were huddled around each other in our parkas and coats, studying the latest card and its strange symbols.

Jack spoke up. "Where is the other card, Dallas?"

"In the house."

"Can you get it?"

I ran for it. When we put the two pieces together, it was clear they had originally been the same card, now torn in half. And when they were matched, the four symbols began to look as if they belonged together. Not as if they were the same message, but as if they were all part of the same code.

If we could figure out the code, we might be able to decipher the message.

Jack studied it and then sat back with a satisfied smile, his legs crossed beneath him. "I figured it out."

"What? What? Tell us! Say something!"

"Indian signs."

"Indian signs? What do you mean?"

He pointed at the four symbols, and just as confidently as he could, he nodded again and repeated his decision. "Indian signs. I've studied them at school."

We didn't know what to think. It wasn't like Jack to kid. He did go to a special school for the retarded, and it was logical that they might study Indians and Indian signs. The more we looked at the symbols, the more Indian they appeared.

The more I thought about the man, the more Indian he looked to me. We demanded to know from Jack what the symbols meant.

He shrugged. "I don't know. It was last year. We didn't learn them all. But they are Indian signs. They used these for messages on trails, and they are always in Indian jewelry and crafts."

I checked our encyclopedias at home and didn't find anything, so I couldn't wait to get to the school library the next day. What I found sent me on a personal mission back to the swimming pool at the other school.

The librarian directed me to the proper reference books where I found long lists and charts and graphs of symbols that had been used by American Indians for centuries. When I came across symbols that looked just like the ones the old Indian had scribbled for me, I felt as if I was discovering the new world all over again.

The rattlesnake jaw stood for strength. He must have seen strength in my ability to swim a hundred meters—even though I almost didn't make it.

The thunderbird track meant bright prospects. I had no idea what he meant by that, unless he thought I had a future as a swimmer. But how would *he* know? And why would he care? Surely he was just a local swimming enthusiast, maybe an amateur expert.

The rain clouds stood for good prospects. He must have written that message after seeing me swim one length of the pool at top speed. The crossed arrows, though, they were the most intriguing. They mean friendship.

The question was, was he referring to my friendship with Jack that made me help Jack out and laugh with him after I had run into him? Or was the Indian trying to communicate friendship to me from himself?

I had to find out.

At the school pool, the swimming coach ran his team through its paces. He blew his whistle and barked orders every few seconds. There were guys diving from the board, practicing starts, flips, turns, and all the various strokes. Finally, the coach had a minute for me.

I was afraid to ask about the old Indian. I had just hoped he'd be there and I'd run into him. But he wasn't there, so I just asked the coach about any swimming competition the Baker Street Sports Club might be able to get into.

"Sure, the Amateur Athletic Union state championships are an open meet for individuals, teams, park districts, clubs, whatever. And they have a division for eleven- and twelve-year-olds too. You have to qualify at smaller meets, but we have enough of those right here that you'd have every chance, that is, if you can swim."

"We can't. At least, we never have in competition."

"Don't expect to make it to the state finals then. You'll need a coach."

"I figured that. Are you available?"

The coach laughed. "Oh, no. I have enough coaching responsibilities with the school and the park district and a couple of individual olympic hopefuls."

I nodded. "Where will the state meet be held?"

"You kidding?"

"No, why would I?"

"Right here, son. It'll be the biggest thing to ever hit this pool. We'll probably see every record for every event broken. It's gonna be something. And if you and your Baker Street friends there don't make it, you'll want to come and watch it, won't you?"

"Oh, you bet. Yes, sir. Uh, coach?"

"Yeah."

"Who is that man who comes and watches the swimmers a lot?"

"You mean the old Indian?"

"Yeah! You know him?"

"Know him? 'Course I know him. Everybody in swimming knows him."

"Maybe that's why I don't know him. Who is he?"

"Name's Johnny Cloud. Don't ask me where the Johnny comes from. Johnny himself probably doesn't know. Grew up on a reservation in Arizona, moved to Mexico when he was in high school. Somehow hooked up with a swimming program down there and actually swam for Mexico in the 1956 olympics."

"You're serious?"

"Absolutely. His event was the individual medley, where you swim all four basic strokes yourself."

"Was he good?"

"He didn't get a medal, if that's what you mean. And his records have been broken by young teenage girls by now, but yes, he was good. One of the best. Perfect technique. Almost no natural ability. Virtually self-trained, though he got some coaching down there. Became an olympic coach. Super teacher. Have tried to employ him here. He won't have anything to do with it. Doesn't want to talk about swimming or anything. Just wants to watch.

"Every once in a while he'll applaud for a particularly

strong performance, but otherwise he's expressionless. He lives nearby here. He's on disability or welfare or something. Keeps to himself. I see him around town. He eats by himself at the diner up the street. Walks to the post office. Never talks. Never smiles. Spends a lot of time here. Sad."

"What's wrong with his leg?"

"I dunno. He won't talk about that either. I told him I recognized him. He nodded. I spoke of several of the races I'd seen in which his well-trained Mexican swimmers had competed. They rarely won, but they always showed well and gave evidence of solid teaching and training. He nodded as if pleased that I knew that, but he says hardly anything.

"I told him he could come to any of our meets for free anytime, but he prefers to watch a lot of the practices and pay when he comes to a meet. I quit trying to talk to him. He was too distant, too shy, too awkward, too uncomfortable. I even asked him out to my home once, but he refused. Was nice enough about it but clearly didn't want to come.

"He nods to me from across the pool about everyday, but I can never get close to him. He heads the other way. If you can get next to the guy, more power to ya."

4

Johnny Cloud

Over the next three weeks, I could talk only the six other guys who had gone swimming with me the first time into forming a team to try to qualify for the state AAU meet.

The problem was, Jack would not be convinced that he could learn to swim and would probably be a strong freestyler or even backstroker. So, we had the biggest equipment manager in captivity and six guys who knew how to swim but who had never backstroked, breaststroked, or butterflyed.

The coach at the school said we could come and practice any time the pool was open and his team wasn't there, which left us with just certain afternoons and evenings. And except for directing us to the right books and manuals, the coach didn't have time to help us.

He told us to watch his team for proper technique in the four basic strokes, but that after that we were on our own. Frankly, we were hopeless. The crawl, which most people know as the freestyle, was the only thing we could really do.

But for us to have any chance in competition, we needed to learn the others and become fairly good in them. We didn't want to have six freestylers and a freestyle relay team. That would get us nowhere.

I kept looking for Johnny Cloud, and I left my towel in its usual place in case he wanted to leave me another message. Sometimes I caught sight of him coming in or leaving, but he moved around a lot, and I never knew where he was from one minute to the next. No more messages were left in my towel.

That was too bad, because if Johnny had wanted to leave me a message, he would have found one from me, neatly tucked into the towel. I had printed NEED, and then drew the Indian version of two morning stars. One was a triangle with a face in it and rays coming out the sides, and the other looked like a knotted coupling.

Morning stars signified guidance to ancient Indians, and if Johnny Cloud knew the language—which he clearly did—he would understand what I was asking for. We needed help, needed guidance, needed his expertise. I was certain he had little else to do.

Finally the day came when Johnny found my message. What was most exciting to me was that if he found mine, that meant he was leaving one for me. I saw him near my towel, and I tried to be careful not to let him see that I was looking.

Soon he leaned over and quickly unfolded it. I saw him looking at my note. Then he left. I ran to the towel. He had not left a message. I was stunned. My note must have scared him off. He wouldn't have been looking in my towel if he hadn't had a message to give me.

The next afternoon I carefully laid my towel out on the front row of seats at the shallow end of the pool. Then Bugsy, Ryan, Cory, Brent, Jimmy, and I stood in the pool, trying to help each other get into positions where we could master the three strokes we hadn't been able to understand.

After about a half hour of our goofing around and getting nowhere, Johnny Cloud showed up and sat right next to my towel. I watched to see if he would look for a message or leave one, and he did neither.

That was all right. I was just hoping he'd show up and watch us. It didn't take long before it had to be clear to him that we really needed help. We were doing everything wrong, but I made sure the other guys quit fooling around and got serious so he wouldn't think we were just playing.

We were holding Jimmy up in the water on his back so he could try backstroking and kicking without sinking. He kept flipping over and standing up because he felt so strange on his back. Johnny Cloud had moved up in his seat and was sitting on the edge, watching intently.

When I looked at him, he would look away or stare right through me as if not seeing us. But finally, when all our attempts failed to make Jimmy float and try the backstroke, I looked pleadingly at Johnny. Surprisingly, he waved me out of the way and signaled to us that we should let go and let Jimmy fend for himself.

We were so shocked that we just let go and backed off. Jimmy instinctively thrust his hands way back over his head and began windmilling with them. It wasn't the best form, but when he added his kicking feet, he was propelled sideways across the pool several feet before he collided with a crowd of other swimmers.

"I did it! I was doing it! It works! And it feels great! Let me try it again with the strokes right!"

He waded back over to us and just laid out on his back by himself. He was calmer this time, not jerky and not panicking. He was threading his way through the water on his own, relaxed and confident. He stopped, turned around, and came back. "You guys can try it, but it's my event."

I looked back at Johnny to thank him. But he was gone.

Cory spotted him at the other end of the pool still watching us. "There he is."

I grabbed Bugsy. "Try the butterfly!"

Bugsy dropped to where the water was up to his neck and started bobbing. He windmilled his arms out of the water, creating a giant splash, and his feet kicked like a frog's legs. Bugsy seemed to go nowhere, despite all the effort.

I looked imploringly to the other end. Johnny held up two

29

fingers and mimicked Bugsy's leg kick style, waving a "no" with his other hand. Then he put the two fingers together and made them undulate like a dolphin's tail.

I nearly went under trying to get to Bugsy. "Change your leg kick from frog style to dolphin style!"

He tried it. Suddenly, he was moving too. What was left? The difficult breaststroke. Would Johnny watch? Would he help? No. He was leaving. I leaped from the pool. I wanted to know where he went. Where he lived. I wanted to talk to him, even if I had to follow him home.

I ran slipping and sliding into the locker room, toweling myself off as fast as I could and drawing glares and shouts from adults. When I was half dressed I charged out into the hall to see if Johnny was still in the building.

He was all the way down the other end of the corridor, on his way out the door. If I hurried. . .

I skipped back into the locker room and whipped on my shoes and socks, then slung my coat over my shoulders as I raced out. Luckily, there was still snow on the ground, though the temperature was still a little above freezing.

My hair was still wet, but my stocking cap was pulled all the way down. I felt damp and cold, but I was on a mission. I wanted to find out where Johnny lived. Even more, I wanted to talk to him.

I followed his tracks, just like an Indian scout, until they joined several others on the busy street in front of the school. I could only guess which way he went, and I sprinted that way, knowing he had a bad leg.

Two blocks away I saw a big, shadowy figure make a right turn. It had to be him. I kept running, gasping for breath and feeling the icy wind dig deep into my lungs. I called after him. "Mr. Cloud! Sir! Wait!"

But it was windy, and the traffic was noisy. And the old man had to have a hat on over his ears, didn't he? I hadn't noticed.

When I caught sight of him again he was entering the front

door of a four-story apartment building. His hands were thrust deep into his pockets. He was wearing a hat, but it didn't cover his ears. His only coat was a leather jacket with a fur collar. I guessed he didn't have gloves. His boots were real waffle-stompers, cookie cutting deep patterns in the snow. The limping foot track had a different look.

I knew that by the time I got to his building he would already be in his apartment. I was right. I skidded up to the door, stopped, took a deep breath, and pulled it open. I found myself inside a tiny glassed-in lobby not much bigger than a phone booth.

The inner door was locked, but there were several mailboxes with names and buttons on them, also a small speaker for an old-fashioned intercom. On a plastic strip I read J. CLOUD, 315B. I pushed the buzzer and held my hand on the door knob, hoping he would buzz me in.

But why would he? He hadn't seen me follow him. The response came through on the staticky speaker. "Who is it?" The voice was gruff but not mean.

"Uh, sir, my name is Dallas O'Neil and—"

"I'm not interested in anything. Thank you."

"But Mr. Cloud, sir, I'm not selling anything."

"Then what do you want?"

"I'm the one from the swimming pool. With the red, white, and blue towel. I've been trying to learn the swimming strokes with my friends. I was wondering if I could talk to you."

I let go of the button, not knowing what else to say and having no idea what he would say. I listened for several seconds. Twice it sounded as if he had depressed his speaker button and had maybe even taken a breath to speak. I prayed he wouldn't send me away.

Just when I had resigned myself to the fact that he was not going to answer, the door buzzed. I was so surprised I almost didn't react quickly enough. In fact, it had quit buzzing, and I opened it in that split second between the buzzing and the automatic switch shut off.

31

I bounded up the stairs to the third floor and turned right. All the apartments to the right were A's, so I hurried back the other way. I found 315B and half expected the door to be open or Johnny to be in the hall waiting for me. I mean, he had buzzed the door. He had to know I was coming.

I knocked lightly on the door. Nothing. I knocked louder. Still nothing. Maybe he had changed his mind. Maybe he was deaf. Maybe he was sick or hurt or busy or listening to the radio. Maybe he hoped I would just go away. I decided not to knock again, but just as I turned to step away, the door opened.

He wasn't standing in the doorway, but it was wide open. I called out his name. Hearing nothing, I stepped carefully inside.

5

First Meeting

The short hallway inside his apartment was dark, and I had the eerie feeling he was there where I couldn't see him, all deeply dark and invisible in the low light.

I was aware of photographs in frames on the wall to my right and closet doors on my left, but I kept walking toward the light, which streamed in through a yellow curtain in the living room. As I got to the end of the hall, my view of the light was temporarily blocked and I jumped.

Johnny Cloud had indeed been in the hallway the whole time, and without greeting me, he had led me into the living room, only coming into view when he blocked the light.

The place was a mess. Stuff was piled on the couch and chairs, and there wasn't much room for the few sticks of furniture he had. On the walls, however, was the story of his life.

He had tossed his coat over the back of a chair, and when he didn't offer to take mine, I did the same. Finally, he looked at me. There was still no expression. The same blank look as always. "You read, then we'll talk."

I liked that idea. I heard him in the kitchen, rummaging in the refrigerator, and I hoped he didn't feel obligated to feed or water me. I heard him set two glasses on the table and pour. I hoped he knew I was too young for beer or liquor.

I could see he had his clippings arranged in order of time, so I stepped back down the hall and turned on a light. It couldn't have been stronger than fifteen watts and didn't help much, but I could make out that he had been an excellent swimmer as far back as high school.

The headlines told of his moving from the reservation to Mexico, then the school and local papers began chronicling his swimming and coaching successes. Finally, he became Mexican olympic swimming coach.

I began to feel rude and went out into the tiny kitchen. He sat before two glasses of Coke. His hadn't been touched. He pointed to a chair, and I wondered if anyone else had ever been in that apartment but him.

The school swim coach had said he couldn't get the man to talk about himself. I assumed from that that he had never got next to Johnny. To my surprise, he spoke first. "You like Coke?"

I shrugged and took a swallow. "You like swimming?"

He still wouldn't smile. But he nodded. "Not to swim or coach anymore. Just to watch."

I stood and stepped toward him, thrusting out my hand. "Name's Dallas O'Neil. I run a club, the Baker Street Sports Club, and we're trying to learn to be competitive swimmers."

I shook his hand hard, the way I'd been taught, but his big hand remained limp. I was afraid maybe he had some sort of other injury and that I was causing him pain to squeeze that hard. I had only been trying to show him how strong I was and how glad I was to meet him.

He squinted. "Johnny Cloud. You can call me Johnny. A tip for you. The Indian does not shake hands hard with a stranger. Might be rude."

"Oh, I'm sorry, I didn't mean to—"

He held up both hands. "It's OK, Dallas O'Neil. I'm just giving you a tip for next time you shake hands with the Indian. Especially this one. We like to defer, to not be presumptuous."

"Was I presump—"

His voice was soft now, though low. "No, no. You only acted as you have been trained. That's good. Good training makes you finish one hundred meters, even though you were ready for only about seventy-five."

I smiled. He remembered. "You thought I wasn't going to make it, didn't you?"

"You almost didn't."

I nodded. He was so wide, so massive. His face was broad. "What would you have done if I had gone under?"

"You did. I almost jumped in."

"Really? That's what you would have done? You wouldn't have called for help?"

He sat still. "I was closest to you. And I can still swim enough to save a foolish child."

That hurt, but I knew it was true. He hadn't said it in a mean way. He meant it. "What did your messages mean, Mr. Cloud?"

He was always slow and deliberate in responding, as if he wasn't used to normal conversation. "You know or you wouldn't have answered."

"But what did you mean by strength and bright prospects and then by good prospects and friendship?"

"Messages mean what they say. It was your strength that carried you all the way back that first day. I thought you had a good future in the sport because of that. Not because of form or talent or technique. But heart."

I beamed, then felt embarrassed. "And the next set of messages? Let me guess. Good prospects meant just about the same as the first message."

Johnny nodded. "But even more now because of technique this time. You were thrashing all about and pushing yourself for only half a race."

"I didn't want the same thing to happen again."

37

"It wouldn't have. You would have paced yourself. You should have tried it."

I felt bad that I hadn't. "But you said again I was a good prospect."

"Not quite. I said good prospects were ahead for you. Maybe."

"And you also gave me the sign for friendship. Does that mean we can be friends?"

Johnny suddenly stood and waved Dallas off. "What would you want to be friends with a broken down old war horse like me for? Nah. No."

I was embarrassed. "But you sent the sign."

"I was referring to you and your retarded friend."

"How did you know he was retarded?"

"Not hard to tell from that distance. Very good, fun-loving, affectionate boy, is he not?"

I nodded.

"And a good athlete, but not in the water, eh?"

I nodded again. How did he know these things?

"He's rangy and coordinated, but I don't know that he could be taught to be comfortable in the water. Many with his problem are not. Many are. But you are close friends?"

"Yes."

"Good."

"I want to be your friend too, Mr. Cloud."

"Johnny!"

"Johnny."

"No, you don't. You want me to coach you."

He was a mind-reader, but he wasn't always right. "I want you to coach us, yes, but I want to be your friend too."

"Why?"

"I don't know."

"That's an honest answer, Dallas O'Neil. You don't know me well enough to know whether you want to be my friend. I have no friends. Only enemies and acquaintances."

"Then you need a friend, sir. Johnny."

"Don't be too sure. Friends have failed me. I am in disgrace in Mexico because we had such a poor showing in the olympics. The Mexicans have never done well in olympic swimming, yet I was disgraced for it."

"How did you get hurt?"

He ignored my question. "There were demonstrations that spilled over into my house. My wife was injured and later died because of the hatred for me. She tried to flee in the car, but the crowd blocked her way and made her crash."

"Is that how you were injured too? Trying to help her?"

He nodded and sat back down but would not look at me. He pointed to his little bedroom, just past my chair. I rose and went in, turning on the light. On the walls in there were the clippings about the demonstration against him, his and his wife's injuries, and her eventual death.

He wasn't banned from Mexico, but it was clear he was no longer welcome there. On the wall by his bed were letters from dozens of U.S. colleges and universities congratulating him on his career and politely refusing his application to join their swim coaching ranks.

It was as if they were badges of honor. Yet, clearly, they had broken his heart. With nowhere to work and nowhere to go, he migrated to this town and moved to within walking distance of a good swimming pool.

The local coach recognized him and had tried to include him, but he was too bitter. Too much had happened. Now he simply lived to watch young swimmers work out. His mind must have quickly calculated their potential, and he must have run through the various training techniques he might use for each.

I returned to find him still at the table, his head down, gazing into his Coke as if it was a hard drink. I had read somewhere of a problem Indians have with alcohol, something about intolerance or their inability to handle even small amounts. I was glad to see no evidence of that in Johnny Cloud's apartment. He was just one terribly sad man.

He didn't seem to notice that I had returned, and I didn't know whether to sit down again or not. I stood waiting. Maybe my visit was over. Maybe he was tired of me. I thought of just leaving.

Finally he looked up. "That's it, isn't it? You want me to coach you, but you don't want to be my friend."

I shook my head, almost unable to speak. "I'd like both, but I'll take one or the other."

He looked at me a long time. "I'll think it over."

"You will?"

"Yes, I will. I will sit and watch you and your friends, and I may try to help you a little. That's all I can promise."

"Will you think about our being friends too, Mr. Cl—uh, Johnny?"

He shook his head slowly. "No, that is something that you'd better think about some more, Dallas."

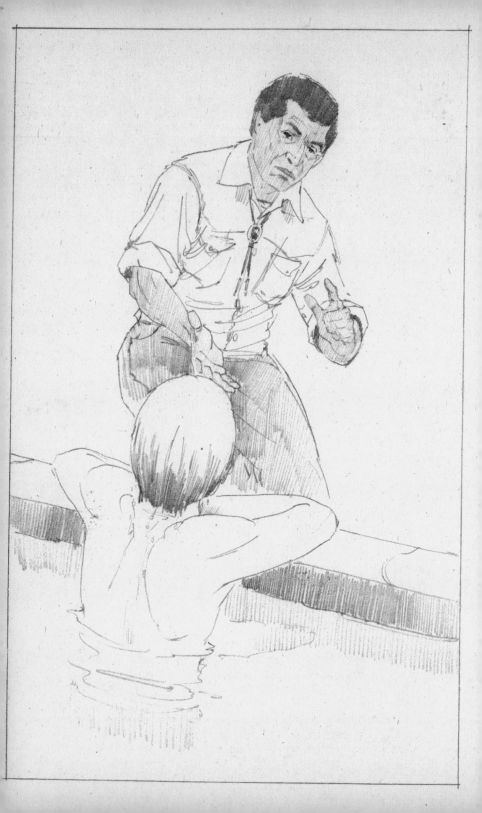

6

The Agreement

What surprised me on my way out of Johnny Cloud's tiny apartment was that he followed me, pulling on his coat and hat again. I hesitated and looked wonderingly at him, but he was volunteering no information and didn't appear to want me to ask where he was going.

He waved good-bye without a word and walked the opposite direction from where I was going. I stopped at the next corner and casually turned to see him stride out of sight, limping as usual.

When he turned, I followed him, staying a block and a half to two blocks behind, careful to not let him see me. He walked to a post office six blocks away. I waited down the street until he came out, clutching a small supply of junk mail and walking back toward his place.

When he was gone, I trotted into the post office. There was only one clerk at the counter. "Did you just wait on Mr. Cloud?"

The old man looked at me warily. "What's it to you?"

"I'm a friend of his. I was just wondering why he doesn't have his mail delivered to his apartment."

"Probably doesn't trust the system is my guess. So what?"

"Well, could I pick it up for him and deliver it to him?"

"If we get a letter from him authorizin' you to. Is that what he wants?"

"I don't know. I sort of wanted to surprise him."

"Nah. No way. Mr. Cloud comes here every day with great hope. He mails something to each of his sons once a week, but he never gets anything back."

"What does he send them? And where?"

"You ask too many questions, kid. How do I know you're a friend of his?"

"I care about him. Trust me."

"Why should I?"

I shrugged. I was getting nowhere and turned to leave. The man called after me. "I wouldn't know what he sends." I turned around to hear him out. "Little packages and letters, that's all. One kid is in Mexico, the other in Arizona. You wanna do somethin' for 'im, write 'im a letter. That's one thing he wants that he never gets."

What a great idea! I would keep in touch with him by mailing letters. On my way back to the school, I went past Johnny Cloud's apartment to make sure of his address. He was shy and quiet, and even if he helped us, I was sure he wouldn't want to talk much, especially about what I wanted to discuss.

I could hardly get the man to talk about swimming, which had been his whole life, let alone about his kids. I had been wondering how in the world I could tell him about God. It seemed impossible until the postal clerk had mentioned writing to him.

I would start slow and easy and friendly, just thanking him for letting me see where he lived and for talking to me. I would tell him that I had thought about what he said and that I would appreciate any help he could give our sports club in swim training. Also, I would tell him that I was sure in the future we would want to be his friends.

I wouldn't wait too long, but I would go slow in talking

about God and Jesus and faith. I didn't want to annoy him or make him think I knew more about life than he did. And I didn't want him to think I thought I was better than he was either. But neither did I want to wait so long that something might happen to him before he had a chance to become a Christian.

Maybe he had faith in God; I couldn't tell. I didn't see any signs, except the symbols he wrote with, that made it look as if he believed in ancient Indian religions. According to the reference books at the library, those symbols could be but weren't necessarily tied to Indian religion either.

My guess was that Johnny Cloud had no interest in God, or, if he did, he'd lost it when he lost his wife. He was such a private person that I didn't know if he would ever talk to me about such personal things, but it was sure worth a try to write to him.

The next Saturday, our six-man team plus Jack made the trek to the swimming pool, hoping to see Johnny and learn a few things. I had mailed him a letter on Thursday, and I had no idea if he had received it yet. In it I had drawn, the best I could, a bear track, a red-cross sized cross, and an arrowhead pointing at the feathered end of an arrow.

My symbols, the best I could figure, meant good omen, paths crossing, and peace. I was trying to say that I thought it was good that our paths crossed and that I hoped we would have a peaceful friendship.

He was there. That made me think he had got it, but nothing he said or did made me sure. He sat near us and watched, and he actually hollered out instructions occasionally. That was more than he had done before.

It was hard to hear him, and we found ourselves wishing he would just come and sit at the edge of the pool. But it was too early in the friendship, if that's what we could call it, for us to invite him. It would have to be in his own time.

There was no message in my towel at the end of the prac-

45

tice, but that didn't mean he hadn't got my letter. With Johnny Cloud you couldn't assume. Something could mean anything or nothing.

It was at our next workout that we knew he had received my letter. He actually waved when we came out of the locker room and into the pool area. I draped my towel over the restraining bar between the spectator seats and the pool and, as was my custom now, strode to the deep end and unceremoniously dived right in.

I swam strong and smooth to the other end, not pushing so hard that I got in trouble, but rather saving myself so I could do my best at a flip turn and swim all the way back to the other end.

I knew my style wasn't the best or strongest, but I tried to glide through the water as if I knew what I was doing. My time wouldn't have been anything spectacular either, because I wasn't pushing.

When I got to the shallow end, I tried my own version of a flip turn and, as usual, hit with only one foot, came up awkwardly, and had to straighten myself out.

When I reached the other end, I looked up at Johnny Cloud. He slowly nodded his head, his chin in his hand. He stood and came around to the edge of the pool and squatted next to where I was dangling in the water from the overhanging lip.

"Catch your breath, then come to the other end."

I should have listened to him. I was so eager to find out whatever it was he wanted to show or tell me that I immediately let go of the wall and began swimming to the shallow end.

I wasn't going fast. In fact, I was swimming a lot slower than I had even the first time, but I hadn't realized how exhausted I was from that first "easy" hundred meters. By half way there I had to stop and dog paddle to rest, and when I got to where my feet touched the bottom, I walked the rest of the way.

Maybe it was just my imagination, but it appeared to me that I had offended Johnny by not listening to him. I should have caught my breath before coming back. Then I wouldn't have had to first dog paddle and then walk like a sissy.

The look on his face seemed to say that I was not a good listener and that he wouldn't have much patience coaching someone like me. For some reason, all I wanted to do was please him and show him that I was a coachable swimmer.

"I should have listened to you. I got tired real quick."

He nodded. "Eagerness to please is a good sign. Eagerness to learn is also good. Prudence, wisdom, a level head are even better. Here, look."

He knelt on his good leg and pointed to the edge of the pool. "The flip turn the good crawlers make only appears to be horizontal. In fact, their feet hit the wall with their bodies turned on their sides in the water. So, one foot is above the other, but both are together at the ankles. Is that a surpise to you?"

I nodded. "Yes, how do they get into that position? When my feet reach for the wall, I hit with only one."

"Don't start your flip turn too far from the end. No good. Lose too much time. And always lead with the hand on your breathing side so you can get one more good gulp of air on your last or second-to-last stroke before going under.

"In a good flip turn, you will bend and tumble and twist the upper part of your body, pushing off with your feet without your hands touching the wall. Whip your lead arm to your waist as you drive your head under water and lower one shoulder. Then follow with the other hand, palms open and facing down.

"Pushing down hard with your hands to help you flip over like a somersault, swing your legs over, but keep them straight. When you are on your side, let your toes and heels glide against the wall and bend your knees to provide the power to push off.

"Now, be very careful that when you push off, you don't

47

stay on your side. Give your upper body another quarter turn as you drive forcefully away from the wall so that you are propelled on your stomach in your normal swimming position.

"Don't breathe right away because in competition everyone else will be turning probably at about the same time, and you might get a mouthful of water from all the waves that are created at the turning end. In fact, see if you can go four or five strokes before coming up for air."

I couldn't wait to try it. "Should I start stroking again as soon as possible?"

He shook his head, and I noticed that the rest of the Baker Street Sports Club team—even Jack—had gathered for the little lecture. "No, as soon as you push off, thrust both arms toward the other end and glide until your speed slows to your normal swimming pace. Any stroking before that will only slow you down. The turn and the start will be the fastest parts of your race because you are pushing off a solid object with your legs. The rest of the time you are trying to do something unnatural: propel a body made for land through water made for fish."

We all laughed, and I saw Johnny Cloud smile for the first time. The way he talked to us and looked at me, I knew he had received my letter.

Jack had a question. "Mr. Cloud, sir, why do you call the freestyle the crawl?"

He smiled again. "Actually, boys, the crawl is the crawl. People who call it the freestyle are incorrect. The freestyle is a competitive swimming event in which you can use any stroke you want. You are free, you see, to use whatever style is fastest for you. There are still some swimmers who will use the butterfly, and I have even seen one or two use the backstroke in the freestyle event. But since the crawl is by far the fastest, most powerful, most speed effective stroke, it has become synonymous with the freestyle."

It was clear that Johnny Cloud was at home, teaching,

coaching, explaining, lecturing. There was a light in his eyes that hadn't been there before. He hustled us back into the water so we could try out our new knowledge.

I had a lot more questions.

7

Real Training

I waded out to where the water was up to my neck and practiced gliding into flip turns several times. When my feet hit perfectly, I would let my knees bend until my heels were almost brushing my seat, then I would explode off the wall and see how far the push took me.

Johnny Cloud was not impressed. "Your flip turns are coming along good, but always work on best stroke possible, even when you think all you're working on is your turns."

I tried, but I was so tired from all the work that I forgot everything I thought I knew about the freestyle, I mean, the crawl. But Johnny was patient. "You're dropping your arms and letting your elbow get below your wrist and shoulder. And sometimes you're locking the elbow and it's not bending at all. You don't want that."

We took a break for a few minutes so he could teach me the best start for the crawl. He told me to spread my feet apart about six inches, gripping the edge of the starting platform with my toes. I was bent over at the waist with my knees also bent slightly and my weight forward on the balls of my feet.

"Be in a tightly wound position so when the gun sounds, you'll be able to spring forward instantly. You can go faster through thin air than you can through thick water, so the farther you leap away from the platform, the farther ahead you'll be. Stay flat, don't dive. Belly flop so you'll be in a position to start your stroke."

Johnny asked me what was strongest, my arms or my legs. "Easy. My legs."

"Right. So what provides most of the thrust in the crawl?"

"My legs."

"Gotcha. Wrong. More than half your forward thrust comes from your arms."

"Why, when my legs are so much bigger and stronger?"

"You need your legs to stabilize you. They are important, and without a good kick, you will fall hopelessly behind. But the arms are most important."

Johnny broke down the arm pull into four parts: entry, glide, pull, and finish. "Fingers enter first! Don't splash! Wrist above fingers, elbow above wrist."

When I got my hands at the proper height and made sure to bend my elbows, I found that in my fatigue I was stroking too wide. Always Johnny would holler, "Too far out from your shoulder line!"

Then I found myself going to the opposite problem, and my arms were crossing over the center line of my body, causing me to roll and tilt. There was so much to remember. Johnny assured me that the more I practiced, the easier it would get. "You will remember everything, and everything will fall together naturally all at once. Let me know when that happens. Then we'll work on speed."

"*Then?* I've been working on it all along!"

He smiled. "All your work on technique has cost you speed. But when it all comes together, the speed will follow."

I shook my head.

He showed me how to roll my shoulder up to the level of my ear, bringing the shoulder out of the water. "Fingers, hand, and elbow into the water in that order!" Even as my arm went out and down, I was to keep it bent. "Head straight, even when the body is rolling!" Johnny told me that unless I was breathing, I should keep my chin tucked into position, right between my shoulders.

"Push your hand down into the water, keeping the fingers together but relaxed. Don't open them, or water will stream through and you will lose pulling power. This is what gives you your pulling force. Once your cupped hand is fully under the water, pull it back under you, making sure it doesn't stray across the middle of your body. If it does, your legs will have to make up for too much rolling, and you will lose balance and speed.

"Push your hand back until your arm is straight, all the way to the thigh. Keep your hand bent at the wrist so you can get one more push against the water before the hand breaks the surface. While one hand is pulling, the other is coming over the top and recovering, getting ready to pull."

I was most surprised at what Johnny taught us about kicking. I thought the best kickers were the ones who sent great splashes from the water, but he said it was better to never break the surface with your feet. "You need all the power you can get, and don't waste action on the air."

We were to see our legs as whips with snapping motions that started at the hips, traveled through the relaxed, bent knees, and ended up at the feet, turned inward and pointed straight back. "The instep will push against the water on the way down, and the bottom of the foot will do the same on the way up."

Johnny advised six kicks to the arm motion, or three for each pull, but he said rhythm was more important than the number. Whatever was most comfortable and effective was what we should stick with.

It was amazing how much faster we were all swimming already.

The toughest thing for me to learn in the crawl was

breathing. I had always breathed on every other stroke, drawing in a huge breath and letting it out slowly as I turned my head back into the water.

Johnny told us to use the air as long as possible, gulping it in and holding it until the last instant, then blowing it out quickly and gulping again. He showed me how I didn't have to open wide, but all I had to do was slightly open the corner of my mouth and take in all the air I needed and wanted from the little air pocket my crawling motion created.

"When racing, you want to hold your breath for a long time sometimes. Otherwise, learn to breathe from either side." I just couldn't do it. I was a left side breather, and I didn't see how I could ever change.

Johnny was insistent. "You must. You need the freedom, the flexibility. There will be times when you have to breathe from either side and not be locked into even or odd strokes. Work, learn, give yourself all the tools you need. You have natural speed that will do you well in all four strokes."

That was the first thing like that he'd said. Suddenly I wanted to master all four strokes, learn to start and turn and stroke and breathe perfectly for each. I wanted to win, to break records, to please Johnny. There was something about the quiet Indian that made all of us want to do that.

Next, Johnny taught Jimmy the best backstroke technique. At first, Jimmy was surprised at the attention. "I thought I was doing pretty good with what you advised the other day."

"You were, but while using your body's natural buoyancy to hold you up, you let your seat drag too low in the water. That slows you down. Arch your back and your seat will come up higher."

We gave Jimmy no end of grief about that.

Johnny Cloud taught him—and the rest of us who watched and listened—how to combine a flutter kick with the windmilling arm motion to create power for speed. "Make sure you reach way back past your head and that your little finger goes in the water first. When the finger hits the water, the other hand should begin coming up out of the water too."

Johnny kept up a good natured holler while Jimmy tried the various techniques. "Tuck in your chin! Tilt your head downward toward your chest!"

The start of the backstroke was fun to watch and learn because it was so different. It was the only stroke that was started with the swimmer in the water.

Johnny had Jimmy grip the gutter of the pool with his back toward the other end. He drew his feet up so his toes curled over the end, and he lifted his body up so his knees were bent and all the pressure was on his hands and feet.

"Head down, chin tucked, feet ten inches apart!"

Jimmy tried it while laughing and lost his grip. He struggled in the water and came up spitting. We howled, but when someone volunteered to take over as the first backstroke student, Jimmy got real serious real quick.

"Hips and feet have to be in the water. Think of yourself as a coiled spring, and breath deeply until you hear me clap. Then go. To your marks, set—" CLAP!

Jimmy threw his arms back but kept his chin tucked. His big legs pushed him forcefully away from the edge, but he hit the water with a thud and began to sink. His arms were flailing, and we were all laughing, but I was afraid we would offend our new, almost, coach, so I shushed everybody.

But Johnny was chuckling too. It was obvious he was enjoying this. He patiently showed Jimmy how to keep his chin down and his head tilted until the start, and then to leap backward, throwing the head and chin back so far that you actually look at the water upside before seeing how far your thrust and glide had got you.

"Everything has to work together, or the start will be weak and a failure. The start is almost everything in the backstroke, all other things being equal. I have seen average swimmers win big upsets with good starts. Good swimmers lose because of a mental lapse."

We pleaded with him. "Tell us. A story. Tell us."

He pulled his shoes off and rolled up his pant legs. Rethinking it, he looked around for the school swim coach and inquired with a nod of the head and a point to the water if it would be OK for him to sit on the side and dangle his feet in the pool.

The coach waved his permission, and it appeared that Johnny was feeling the lukewarm, buoyant pool water for the first time in years. He fell silent, and his eyes had a faraway look. He folded his arms as if he was cold, though he couldn't have been.

As we bobbed and stood in the shallow waters near his feet, he gazed over our heads toward the windows. The late afternoon winter sun made him squint. His nose and cheek bones were bright in the light, and his hair and shoulders were shadowed.

He began slowly in a melancholy monotone. "The Pan American Games, nineteen-sixty. Mexican swimmer named Felipe Feliz. Average backstroker, no national or even team records. Hardly ever a first. But this time he was inspired. By what, I don't know. But that start. I'll never forget it."

8

Johnny's Story

"It was in the semi-finals. Sixteen swimmers were left, and the first four of the two semi heats would advance to the finals. Felipe had the sixteenth best time of the semi-finalists. Merely qualifying would have been a miracle.

"In the first semi, the first four finishers all broke the world record. The better swimmers, we all thought, were in the second semi, Felipe's race. He didn't have a chance. It would likely take another world record to even finish fourth. Felipe had never been closer than three seconds from even the old world record, and in swimming you'll learn that three seconds can be an eternity. In today's finals of the NCAA tournament, there is often less than two seconds between first and twelfth place.

"But when the gun sounded, Felipe blasted from the start, his head rising high above all the others, his back arched, his face upside down staring not into the water but far up the other end of the pool.

"It caused a gasp among the spectators as he seemed to fly off the gun, hands and arms stretched, reaching, reaching. The start alone raised me from my seat. Every eye was upon him. All the fans, all the coaches, all the teams, even—believe it or not—his competitors.

"You'd have had to have been there to believe it. A start like that can be seen in the peripheral vision of every other swimmer. He was like a specter, a hair's breadth from jumping the gun, leaping, exploding through the air.

"He was the last one to hit the water but was so far ahead by the time he did that his wake alone washed over the others and rocked them, nearly threw them off pace. Some actually rolled onto one side to see what had happened—who had jumped in the pool from the side.

"He hadn't. He had merely got the best start in the history of the sport, regardless of stroke. I've seen some good freestyle starts in my day, but this was unlike anything anyone has ever seen, before or since.

"The start energized him. He sliced into the water crisp and neat and began his fluid strokes like a man possessed. He had always had good technique. We stressed that above all else. Dignity, class, professionalism, win or lose.

"He had seldom led in world class competition. He was one of those dual meet champions, an expected conference winner. Always fared well in the national competition but held no Mexican records. On the world scene he had never qualified for a final. He was simply a decent swimmer to fill lane seven or eight in the quarterfinals and sometimes, when he was at his best, the semis.

"Well, he took that sixteenth best time into the semis, and it was forgotten when he speared his way to that best ever start. You couldn't have scripted it better. No one could draw it, animate it, film it in slow motion better. We have a film of it, but I quit watching it after fifteen or so times because I can still see every stroke. It can't be imagined, can't be exaggerated.

"It was as if he were one with the starter pistol. His feet were the first to leave the edge of the pool, his hands the last to break the surface. The adrenaline that shot through his system—when? before that incredible start or because of it?—found its way to his technique.

"I've seen mediocre swimmers jump out to a lucky lead or find themselves ahead at the turn and completely lose it because they got too excited. They got heady. They smelled victory and swam past their abilities.

"But not Felipe. He was conscious of what had happened, sure. He told me that himself. 'Coach,' he said, 'I wasn't sure why it had happened, but I knew it had. I didn't let doubt enter my mind. I just kept stroking, not really feeling that anything at all was different about the race except my lucky start, the kind of start you dream about all your swimming life. Until the turn, that is.'

"Ah, the turn. Felipe led by five meters when he ducked for his flip turn. I knew something was different when not even his knee caps were visible on the surface. He had flipped at top speed, keeping his entire body under, breaking perfectly and firing away from the wall just right.

"He had led all the swimmers into the turn by so far that he didn't have to deal with any turbulence except the man in lane seven as he approached the wall when Felipe was gliding back toward the finish.

"But because he was so low in the water and had pushed off with such force, he didn't resurface until the man in lane seven had passed him and was about to start his own turn. I couldn't believe what I was seeing.

"Felipe surfaced with a lead of yet another four to five meters, and he had not weakened a bit. In fact, because of his start and his turn and his exquisite technique, he had less distance to swim than the others.

"Still, he stayed within himself. He told me later that he was not aware that he was stroking any faster than usual, but in studying the films, we can see that he was actually stroking and kicking more than ten percent faster than normal.

"He just kept pulling away. The favorites, including the former world record holder, turned to see him as he sliced through the water. He distanced himself so far from the rest of the field that his water was smooth and taut.

"Felipe seemed to accelerate as he finished, his hand banging against the touch pad. There was a stunned silence in the pool as spectators stared at the clock. Felipe had shattered the world record and put it out of reach for six years! Unheard of in swimming.

"He was an immediate sensation. He got a lot of congratulations and claps on the back, especially from the superstars, but they hardly knew him by name. He was just 'that Mexican swimmer with the good technique and no speed.' Now he was somebody. The odds-on favorite in the finals.

"In the finals, he finished dead last, despite his second best time ever. He never swam that fast again the rest of his career. A fluke? Yes. Of course. Everyone tried to explain it away.

"But I have seen those films more than a dozen times, and I know he didn't jump the gun. His turn was fair and legal, not to mention as fast as any turn ever.

"No, the fact is, that was Felipe Feliz's moment. Everything, and I mean everything, worked perfectly for him. Even the choice of lane, eight, was right. Not because it always went to the slowest qualifier back then, but because it kept him from turbulence that would have interrupted his record pace.

"Even if his turn had been mediocre or if he had lost his pace near the end, he would have broken the world record. But, no, everything was perfect, and I'll tell you this: I felt privileged to have been there. To have been his coach? Yes. But that day it was as if no one was his coach.

"That day he belonged to history, to fate, to perfection. I did not coach him to such great heights. I knew I would never see so stunningly perfect a performance again as long as I lived, and I have not. There will not likely be another performance like that, and I refuse to disappoint myself by looking for one."

For being a quiet man, Johnny Cloud had indeed gone on.

We hadn't even noticed that we were the only ones left in the pool. Or that the school swim coach had come by and sat in the stands behind Johnny.

Before long, before any of us could find words, Johnny spoke again. "A performance like that, one that transcends all logic, one that comes to embody the essence of the sport itself, should be the goal of every swimmer who specializes in any stroke. Of course, the ultimate would be for someday a medley marathoner to have that kind of a race in every event. A perfect start, a faster pace, killer turns, liquid transitions from one stroke to the next. I will be in heaven before I see that in an individual medley racer."

I wanted to ask him if he really planned to go to heaven and how he was going to get there. I decided to let it wait until I could write him another letter. But I also decided I would not write him two letters in a row. He had to answer my first one before he would get a second.

Johnny slowly pulled his feet from the pool and pivoted on his seat before standing. He kept his pant legs up until his legs drip dried. I think each of us had the idea to offer him our towel, but no one could speak. Not even the school coach. He just slowly walked toward the locker room.

Johnny followed him, several paces back, and none of us said anything. We just watched them leave. The door to the locker room swung open and shut, and the school coach was out of sight. Johnny stopped and rolled down his pantlegs, then found his coat and headed out into the early evening bitterness.

It had grown dark while he talked. No one swam. No one roughhoused. No one laughed or even smiled. We thought our own thoughts, dreamed our own dreams, vowed our own vows, and slowly pulled ourselves from the pool. Some climbed the ladder, others just hoisted themselves over the side.

We showered and dried and dressed in silence. I thought I knew what the others were thinking but I wasn't sure. If they were thinking what I was thinking, they were choosing their specialty, their stroke.

They were committing themselves to give whatever it would take to get in shape, learn the technique, and be the best they could be. They were deciding to one day swim a race like Felipe Feliz had, one that made Johnny Cloud proud to have simply been at poolside.

We learned a lot about Johnny that afternoon. And I learned a lot about myself. I wanted to get next to this man, really get next to him. I didn't know if he'd be embarrassed by having told the story, or whether he'd want me to bring it up again, or what.

All I knew was, I wanted to become a great swimmer, at least the best I could be. I wanted Johnny as my coach, and I wanted to swim the individual medley relay.

Even more than that, I wanted to keep writing to Johnny Cloud. And I wanted to introduce him to God.

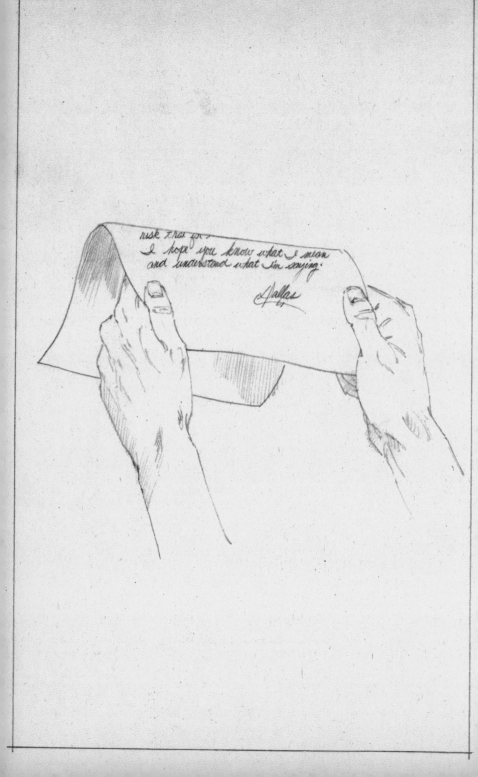

9

Evolving into a Team

The toughest lesson for the Baker Street Sports Club that winter was to learn that we were not ready for competition. Coach Johnny Cloud became much more open and friendly and helpful, but he was also painfully honest.

I was eager to see us enter some meets, just to see how we stacked up against other kids our own age. But he wouldn't let us. "If I am going to be your coach, I will tell you when you are ready. I am timing you, and believe me you are not ready. Your times are so far from competitive for your ages that it would do you no good to be beaten so soundly."

I wasn't sure I agreed with that. "But wouldn't we learn about starts and turns and competition and swimming before spectators?"

He nodded thoughtfully. "Perhaps. But not yet. I promise I will enter you in one small meet, maybe even a school meet, before the two qualifying meets leading to the state championships."

We looked forward to that as if for Christmas.

Cory became our butterflyer, Jimmy our backstroker, Bugsy our breaststroker, and Ryan, Brent, and I our freestylers. The problem was, we needed one more freestyler because we wanted to enter several events.

We would all swim the 100 and the 200 in each of our specialties, and I would enter the individual medley, fifty yards of each stroke. We would also have a medley relay with our best person at each stroke. But for the 200 freestyle relay, we needed four freestylers. One of the other guys might be able to double up and also become proficient in the crawl, but no one seemed interested.

Meanwhile, I was writing regularly to Johnny Cloud. He answered sometimes by mail, sometimes by leaving little notes in my towel, and sometimes by actually mentioning my letters in person.

That was always the most surprising, because since his long story about the wonderful backstroke world record by Felipe Feliz, he had become very quiet again. Now when he spoke, he spoke mostly to me and to Jack.

For some reason, he really took to Jack. He gave the big kid just as much personal attention and instruction as he gave the rest of us. Jack loved it, and he loved talking to Johnny. There were times when I wished I could talk to the old coach as easily.

In the letters, I had started to tell him about my faith. Being careful not to preach or offend him in any way, I followed my Sunday school teacher's advice and simply told him my own story, how I had seen my need for forgiveness of my sin and how God had provided that through the death of Jesus on the cross.

I wrote that Jesus had risen from the dead and promised us eternal life—and that He left us the Holy Spirit to give us power over sin in our lives. "Johnny, I just wanted to tell you this because it makes me so happy. I have peace, and I'm also secure about the future. I know I have life that will never end."

In a return letter, Johnny told me he believed in God and in the afterlife, but that he also believed that there were many ways to God. "My way is to do the best I can, try not to hate, to be bitter, to be angry. I try to work hard to please God, and then, Whoever He is, I will be safe."

I wrote back, "But do you feel safe? Or is there a nagging feeling that you can never do enough to please God, that nothing you do in your own power can match His perfection? Are you good some days and not others?"

He said I made some sense, and he agreed there was a lot of truth to what I said. "I have studied Jesus and believe He was a very fine, very good teacher and moralist. I do not believe He rose from the dead or is God."

It was painful to receive the letter in which he said that, but in a way I was glad to know where he stood. I did not accept the fact that he was rejecting my witness or, worse, finally deciding against Christianity. He was clear, though, about where his mind was at that point.

I didn't give up. I kept writing, kept thanking him for coaching us, kept assuring him of my prayers that his sons would one day make contact with him again and that they would be able to forgive one another for whatever had happened between them.

And then I tried the best logic I knew about his feelings about Jesus. "Your thoughts about Him make sense up to one very important point. That point is that Jesus Himself said He was the only way to God. He said He was the way, the truth, and the life and that no one could come to God except through Him. Another place He said, 'I and my Father are one.'

"So, it's all right for you to not believe that, if you choose. I cannot make up your mind for you, and Jesus Christ won't force you into His everlasting kingdom. But don't you agree that you can no longer hold Jesus in such high esteem?

"Would you say that a man was a good teacher and moralist if he claimed to be something he was not? What would the Baker Street Sports Club think of you if you started saying you and God were one, or that you were the only way to God?

"Would we look at your brilliant coaching and example and background and say, 'Well, he's a good teacher'? No, we would say, 'Stay away from this man. He's a nut. He thinks he's God.

"With all respect, Johnny, I don't think you can have it both ways. Jesus cannot be a good teacher unless He is who He says He is. If He is not, then at best He's crazy. At worst, He's a liar. Of course, my view is that He is exactly who He says He is.

"Would you do me a favor? If I sent you a book, would you read it? It's the four Gospels in modern English, easy to read. I know you can read even difficult material, but you might find this more enjoyable than old English.

"I won't bring it to you unless you ask, because the last thing I want to do is push you. I don't want to offend you either, but I'll risk that for the sake of your eternal soul. I hope you know what I mean and understand what I'm saying."

His response was quick. He spoke to me in person at practice the next day. "Don't worry about offending me. I have a lot to learn, a lot to consider. If I believed what you believed, I would feel the need to tell everyone and make sure they all decided what they were going to do about the afterlife. Don't think I don't appreciate it, even if you haven't convinced me yet."

"I could never convince you, Johnny. That's not even my job. My job is to tell you. It's the job of the Spirit to convince you. Only God can do that."

He nodded, but he was through talking. At the end of practice, he said he would read the book if I brought it. I brought it the next day.

Soon we were ready for our first meet. There was a triangular meet of junior high teams scheduled for the pool in which we practiced. The coach said that he could just as easily add our team and make it a quadrangular meet, allowing two entrants from each team in each event.

70

Johnny had a surprise for us. "Jack is going to compete."

"In what?"

"The freestyle relay. He's going to start, because that will be less confusing for him. If he had to wait for someone to touch the wall before beginning, he could get confused or panic. This way, all we have to do is coach him to be ready to hear the gun. Brent will go second, Ryan third, and Dallas fourth."

Well, it was pitiful. We finished dead last in every event, but we sure learned a lot. Cory jumped the gun in the butterfly and then held back too long the second time. He went out much too fast and found himself almost unable to finish.

But he learned what it was like to swim in competition, before hundreds of screaming fans and next to swimmers who tried every psychological trick in the book to scare you. Some scowled at him, some ignored him, some bragged in front of him, some threatened him.

That's not a smart thing to do to Cory. Before he was a Christian, he would have just as soon popped a guy for threatening him. Or he might have sworn at him and threatened him right back.

But now all he did was talk to the threatening one as if he had a problem. The guy sidled up to Cory and sneered at him. "I'm gonna wipe the pool with you, fool."

Cory smiled at him. "You're that good a swimmer?"

The other kid nodded. "You'd better believe it."

"Well, I don't."

"Yeah? Well, you'll find out."

"How? By your telling me or by your showing me in the pool?"

"Both!"

Cory shook his head slowly. "Nope, not both. Talk is cheap. Nothing you tell me will prove anything to me. And if you were as good as you say you are, you wouldn't have to say anything, would you? You must be pretty worried or insecure about your ability."

71

Cory was talking quietly, evenly. It drove the guy nuts. In the race, the big mouth finished second and smacked his hands in the water and swore. Cory swam over to him. "You beat me, but you didn't get first place. You still wanna wipe the pool with me?"

Jimmy was last in the backstroke too, but he had a good start and was about fourth at the turn. He lost stamina too, but he was only a stroke away from seventh place. Johnny was pleased. "Good prospects."

Bugsy did well in the breaststroke, though he too finished eighth. He was several seconds ahead of his best practice time, and Johnny was nearly jumping around. "You come alive in competition, Bugsy! The more you compete, the more you will improve. You can win some meets someday."

I did better than my best practice time by several seconds too, and I felt I learned a lot. I wasn't so intimidated by the meet and the competition my second time up to the starting platform, and that was what I was looking for.

But the freestyle race is so fast, and the other swimmers had so much training and experience, I really never had a chance. Losing by quite a bit, in spite of swimming my personal best time ever, made me realize how much I had to grow to be able to compete.

The freestyle relay was coming up, and we all looked forward to Jack's first experience in the water in a real contest.

10

Finally Getting Somewhere—Almost

The freestyle relay was unbelievable. Johnny Cloud had worked so long and hard with Jack on his starts that when the gun sounded, Jack leaped out to a lead.

He nearly turned in his lane to see how he was doing compared to everyone else, but we were all screaming at him, telling him to just keep driving and stay ahead.

Jack didn't know how to do a flip turn. That was why he was in the 200 freestyle relay. He didn't have to do a flip turn. All he had to do was get to the other end of the pool as fast as possible. And he did.

He was actually in first place when he touched the wall and Brent dove in. Almost immediately, two other swimmers passed Brent, but he did fairly well. He had got away far enough ahead of everyone else that he had been able to dive into fairly smooth water.

He was light and not powerful, but he glided along pretty well, finishing his heat tied for third when Ryan dived in. He was our weakest man, and it was supposed to be up to me to make up whatever he lost when I swam the anchor leg.

At first, Ryan didn't appear to be losing any ground. He

stayed with the first four swimmers for about twenty-five meters, then finally started to drop back. He fell to sixth, and then seventh.

As I waited for him to touch, I could hardly stand the tension. Even though I knew I was one of the weakest freestylers in the meet, I felt good. I felt as if I could do much, much better this time. I watched the other swimmers tiring, and I knew their anchormen, supposedly the fastest swimmers on each team, would be fast.

I just wanted Ryan to touch before he fell to last place. If he was still in seventh, I was certain I could pick up a place, maybe two. Wouldn't it be great to get a fifth place in the relay?

I leaned over on the takeoff platform and let my arms hang. The closer he got, the more taut I made them, tensing my legs and bending at the knees, ready to spring into action. As he came beneath me, I leaned way over and when he touched, I exploded off the board.

My arms were a little late in reacting, and as I descended toward the water, I threw them out ahead of me and arched my back. My feet and hands separated from each other, and I belly flopped painfully, my body at an angle in the lane.

My first order of business was to straighten myself out, but I had already trained myself to begin stroking as soon as I felt water. I didn't want to let anyone catch me, and, in fact, I wanted to catch the number six swimmer and—I hoped—the number five man as well.

So there I was in the water, swimming almost sideways, feet and hands uncoordinated, flailing and splashing and thinking I was at least keeping our position. In truth, I was suddenly in last place.

I felt the rope and the plastic buoys brush my body and I knew if I wasn't careful, I'd be disqualified. Maybe that would have been better than finishing last, but in a panic, I slowed and straightened myself, then got all my parts moving together again.

It felt better that way, and I knew I was in my natural rhythm. But I was swimming slower than usual, and everyone was pulling away. I tried to pick up the pace, only to realize that I had held my breath during that whole ordeal.

I gasped for a supply of air and kept swimming, but I had gone too long without oxygen. My arms and legs felt like lead. My breath was short, my heart raced. This was just a fifty-meter leg in a freestyle race. There was no threat of my being in real danger, but now I wondered if I could even finish.

I sneaked a peek at the other swimmers and realized they were mostly finishing. First and second touched a second apart, and the others were straggling in. I was still struggling.

I sensed my teammates watching and worrying, and I even caught a glimpse of Johnny limping along the poolside, staring and concerned. And puzzled. I knew if I started to go down, a lot of people could save me, but I just couldn't let that happen.

I was the anchorman, the captain of the Baker Street Sports Club, Johnny's favorite swimmer, his friend. I couldn't humiliate him like that. It was bad enough he had to coach a whole team of losers. I couldn't let us lose a race by default.

I summoned all my courage and strength and prayed for a little more. The end seemed to be moving farther from my reach as I labored toward it, but I knew that was just my imagination.

I settled into a stroking rhythm I could handle and found myself, finally, turning freely and regularly in the water. My stroke was fluid, my breathing regular, my heart rate slowed. Of course, so did my pace, and I would wind up with the slowest time of the four of us on the freestyle relay team.

When I finally touched and hung on to rest, I heard the polite applause. It grew louder, as if the crowd and my teammates and opponents realized that my simply finishing was a feat in itself. Other swimmers had quit in similar situations, and I said a prayer of thanks that that hadn't happened.

Johnny helped me out of the pool. "Can you recover in time for the individual medley?"

I told him honestly that I didn't know. "I thought I was going to die there for a minute."

"So did I." I could tell by the look on his face that he meant it.

"You wouldn't have let me drown."

He shook his head. "Of course not."

Strength began to return as I sat at the edge of the pool. "At least I know where I'd go if I died."

He looked at me sharply. "And I don't?"

"I didn't say that, Johnny. I didn't mean anything about you."

"But I don't. I don't know for sure where I'm going when I die."

"Keep reading that book, and you can. You know that, don't you?"

"I have started reading it. It does seem to promise answers."

I paced around the side of the pool a couple of times, hoping more strength would return and that my memory of the fear would go away. I still felt humiliated, but my teammates were kind.

I had two events to go. There was the medley relay, where I would swim the last fifty freestyle. And there was the individual medley, where I would swim all four strokes, fifty meters each. That was the one I was sure I was not ready for.

And I wasn't. I wish I could say I was. I wish I could say that by some miracle I became the best swimmer in the meet and grabbed a medal for us. The truth is, I had nothing left and neither did any of my teammates.

By the time I was ready to swim my fifty freestyle at the end of the relay, we were so far behind that the first place team was just ten meters from the finish. Johnny hurried over to me. "Pace yourself. This is just training. Don't try to make up *any* ground, and I mean it. This is just to practice your start and then a nice, easy fifty. OK!"

I started to shake my head, but I knew better. That individual medley was coming up, and if I had a hope of even finishing that, I would have to save myself here. "Maybe you should sub someone for me."

"Too late. You're booked, and here comes Bugsy."

I turned back and waited for him to touch. And then I did just what Johnny said, not because it was such good advice—though, of course, it was—but because I didn't have any choice.

I might have been able to start a little faster than I did, but I would have lost all stamina immediately, so I didn't push. I calmly and casually stroked through my fifty, finishing a good twenty seconds behind the seventh place finisher.

Surprisingly, when I emerged from the pool, I felt almost refreshed. My tightness was gone. My fatigue, my pain, my shortness of breath. I felt loose. Relaxed. In half an hour, I would be ready for the individual medley.

But Johnny had other ideas again. He sat with me far away from the rest of the action. "I think you should take it easy in the medley too."

"But why? I feel good. And I'll fall so far behind that it'll be embarrassing."

"That will be good for your character. If this last one didn't bother you, that won't either. What you need is experience in this type of race, this type of meet. You proved in the freestyle relay that you weren't really ready. Now just run through the paces on this and try to finish. It will be much, much more difficult than you think."

I sat staring, thinking. "Really?"

He nodded.

"But I feel so good."

"I know. But tell me. What do you really feel like doing right now with this warm, mellow feeling? That's what it is, isn't it?"

I nodded.

"What does it make you want to do?"

"Win the medley."

"You want to win, sure, but if you could do anything you wanted to do right now, anything at all right this instant, what would it be?"

I thought a moment. "Eat."

He nodded knowingly. "Just as I thought. You're exhausted. You'd like a big meal and then a long nap."

I couldn't argue with him. "Exactly."

"Then swim the I.M. easy and do just that."

I still wasn't convinced, but by the time I got to the starting platform, I was. My peaceful, easy feeling had deteriorated to the point where I could hardly walk. I was yawning, stretching, feeling lazy.

When the gun sounded, I started fast and strong, but on my second or third butterfly stroke, I settled into an easy rhythm and let the rest of the field speed away from me. My coach knew best.

11

The Last Message

Even with my very slow pace, the individual medley was strenuous. Coach Cloud had been right all along. It was all I could do to finish. I wasn't in trouble, not panicking or sinking or out of breath.

Just exhausted. My muscles tightened, but I kept going. I quit doing flip turns, and my technique went down the drain. It was a strange experience, chugging along while everyone else was working so hard.

Doing the butterfly so slowly must have looked strange in the water. My arms first came too high out of the water and splashed a lot, then I could hardly get them out of the water at all.

Switching to the backstroke was relaxing at first, but there is some effort required in just staying above the water, especially if you lack the strength to keep your back arched.

The breaststroke was the worst. In fact, it was the one stroke that Johnny almost discouraged us from trying in the early stages of our racing careers. It takes more energy than any of the other strokes, and it is also the slowest. It was torture.

By now I was totally convinced of Johnny's wisdom, and I was no longer trying to prove anything. I just wanted to endure, to survive, to finish, above all else. Even the thought of fifty more meters of freestyle just about did me in.

The freestyle is the easiest, but when I finally switched to that, it didn't seem easy at all. There is always a tendency to push harder when you have an easier stroke, but that temptation somehow passed me by.

I had just begun the crawl when I realized I was the last swimmer in the pool. A great roar rose up. This was the last of the individual races, and there was no one anywhere to watch but me.

Apparently everyone could see I was a beginner who really had no business in that type of competition. But I was finishing, and they felt that deserved encouragement. Under any other circumstances, I might have risen to new heights with all eyes on me and all hands clapping, all voices cheering.

But when I say there was nothing left, I mean nothing. I wanted to spring a little, turn on a little power, maybe at the very end, just to let the crowd know I appreciated it. But when I reached down for a little something extra, I came up empty.

By the time I finished and the crowd rose to its feet, I didn't have the strength to even wave or lift my head and smile. I hung there in the pool, one arm draped over the side to keep me from sinking like a rock, and my head was lowered to my chest.

My teammates finally had to help me from the pool. I wondered if I ever wanted to follow through on my vow to be a great swimmer some day, to impress Johnny Cloud, to strive for a performance like Felipe Feliz had accomplished years before.

If nothing else, that day and that final race made me appreciate even more what competitive swimmers go through to sacrifice their bodies and their minds to athletic excellence.

Two weeks later, a much more realistic, much more disciplined Baker Street Sports Club swimming team entered the first of two qualifying meets for the state finals. If you qualified here, you advanced to the next meet. If you qualified there, you went to the state AAU meet.

We had little hope, but Johnny had some strategy. He allowed us each to choose only one event. What a great idea. It forced us to think as a team.

For instance, if we chose the medley relay, that meant that none of the four of us in that event could swim in any of the individual events. All seven of us wanted to compete, so here's what we decided upon:

Cory, Jimmy, Bugsy, and I would enter the medley relay. Jack, Ryan, and Brent would enter the individual freestyle events, the 50, the 100, and the 200. Before the meet, I asked Johnny what he really thought our chances were.

"Honestly?"

I nodded.

"Nil."

"Really? Nothing for anyone?"

"One chance."

"Who? The relay team?"

He shook his head.

"Who, Johnny? I just want to see how good a predictor you are."

"Jack."

"In the fifty free?"

He nodded. "Best chance. Big man. Strong. Enthusiastic. If he gets a good start, he could at least qualify for the quarter-finals. His times in practice have been within a second of qualifying him."

"But a second is a long way off here."

"I know. I told *you* that, remember? But with the excitement of the meet, the crowd, the competition—and with Jack's ability to tune out all the distractions, well, you never know."

I thought for a moment. "Johnny, are you going to coach us next year?"

"You want me to?"

"'Course! Sure, yeah."

"I wouldn't miss it for anything. I like you boys. You work hard. You love the sport. You care."

"And do we have potential? I mean really, tell me the truth."

"Unlimited."

"And you're not just saying that?"

"You know me better than that."

He was right. I did. I shouldn't have even asked the question. I nodded. "And where are you in your reading?"

He looked uncomfortable, but the time had come to be blunt, to push a little, to force the issue. "I will leave you a message."

"In my towel?"

"Same as always."

Knowing that and wondering what it could possibly be that he wanted to tell me made the meet go slowly. Our relay team did well but didn't qualify. It felt so good not to finish last. We all improved on our individual times, and Ryan and Brent finished fifth and sixth in their qualifying heats in the free-sytle.

Jack was superb, just as Johnny had predicted. He won his qualifying heat with his best time ever, and other coaches began demanding to see his birth certificate. Fortunately, we had thought to bring it along.

In the quarterfinals, he finished fourth, just barely qualifying for the semi. Somehow, in the semi, he finished fourth again, which isn't supposed to happen. In the final, he finished fifth and missed going to the state qualifier meet by one place.

He was so happy he was grinning and laughing. And in fact, we could hear him laughing sometimes as he swam, he loved it so much.

The other teams were throwing their coaches in the pool at the end of the meet, but that didn't seem the right thing for us to do to Johnny. He was older, and he had the bad leg. And anyway, that wasn't our style, or his.

We just surrounded him and applauded him. And while the rest of us kept clapping, one by one each member of the team stepped forward and shook his hand. When Jack shook his hand, Johnny embraced him, and I thought I saw tears in his eyes.

He promised to coach us next year, and somehow we knew it would be a different story next time. We would be older, bigger, wiser in the ways of swimming. We had learned some hard lessons. Swimming was unlike most sports that you can just pick up and become good at with a little practice. It takes a total commitment, and there's no end of competition.

I waited while the rest of the guys gathered up their stuff, then I waited until Johnny had left. I slowly walked to my towel and checked around for his note. It was on a full sheet of paper this time.

At the top he had written THANKS. At the bottom he had signed his full name. In the middle, he had drawn several symbols, and I winced as I realized I would have to run to the library to figure them all out.

He had drawn a tepee on a small globe. Above it, high over the clouds, he had drawn a hogan wheel. Between the earth and the wheel, he had drawn saddle bags and a sky band. Off to the right, as if to sum it all up, he drew an ornate butterfly.

No one knew where I had gone, but I didn't have time to tell anyone. I raced to the library and still had my coat and hat on as I searched through the reference section that had contained the Indian symbols. I couldn't believe it. It was gone.

I hurried to the librarian. "One of your reference books is missing, and no one is supposed to take it out of the library."

She shushed me. "No one can take it out without tripping an alarm. All our books are protected that way. If it's not in place, it may have been misplaced, or someone else may be using it."

I hadn't thought of that. I skipped back and looked to see if it was in some other spot. No. Then I looked at all the desks where student and adults were looking at reference works. Sure enough, a middle-aged man had the book I needed.

I hung around, looking as impatient as I was, and if he noticed me it probably only made him slower to return it. But finally he did.

I tore through it to the page with the Indian symbols. The tepee stood for a temporary home. The sky band meant "leading to happiness." The saddle bags indicated a journey. The hogan wheel meant "permanent home."

So, earth was his temporary home. His journey to happiness would take him to heaven, his permanent home.

And the butterfly? At first I thought it had something to do with swimming, maybe the stroke he wanted me to master for next year.

But in Indian symbols, the butterfly means "everlasting life."

Johnny Cloud had made his decision. He was a Christian. I had to get home. There was an important letter to write.